My Own Home

by Lyn Littlefield Hoopes

illustrated by Ruth Richardson

A Charlotte Zolotow Book
An Imprint of HarperCollins*Publishers*

My Own Home
Text copyright © 1991 by Lyn Littlefield Hoopes
Illustrations copyright © 1991 by Ruth Richardson
Printed in the U.S.A. All rights reserved.
1 2 3 4 5 6 7 8 9 10
First Edition

Library of Congress Cataloging-in-Publication Data
Hoopes, Lyn Littlefield.
    My own home / by Lyn Littlefield Hoopes ; pictures by Ruth
Richardson.
        p.   cm.
    "A Charlotte Zolotow book."
    Summary: One foggy day, a lost little owl finds out what home is
when he realizes that he is already there.
    ISBN 0-06-022570-X. — ISBN 0-06-022571-8 (lib. bdg.)
    [1. Owls—Fiction. 2. Animals—Fiction.] I. Richardson, Ruth,
date ill. II. Title.
PZ7.H7703My 1991   90-4386
[E]—dc20   CIP
                                                         AC

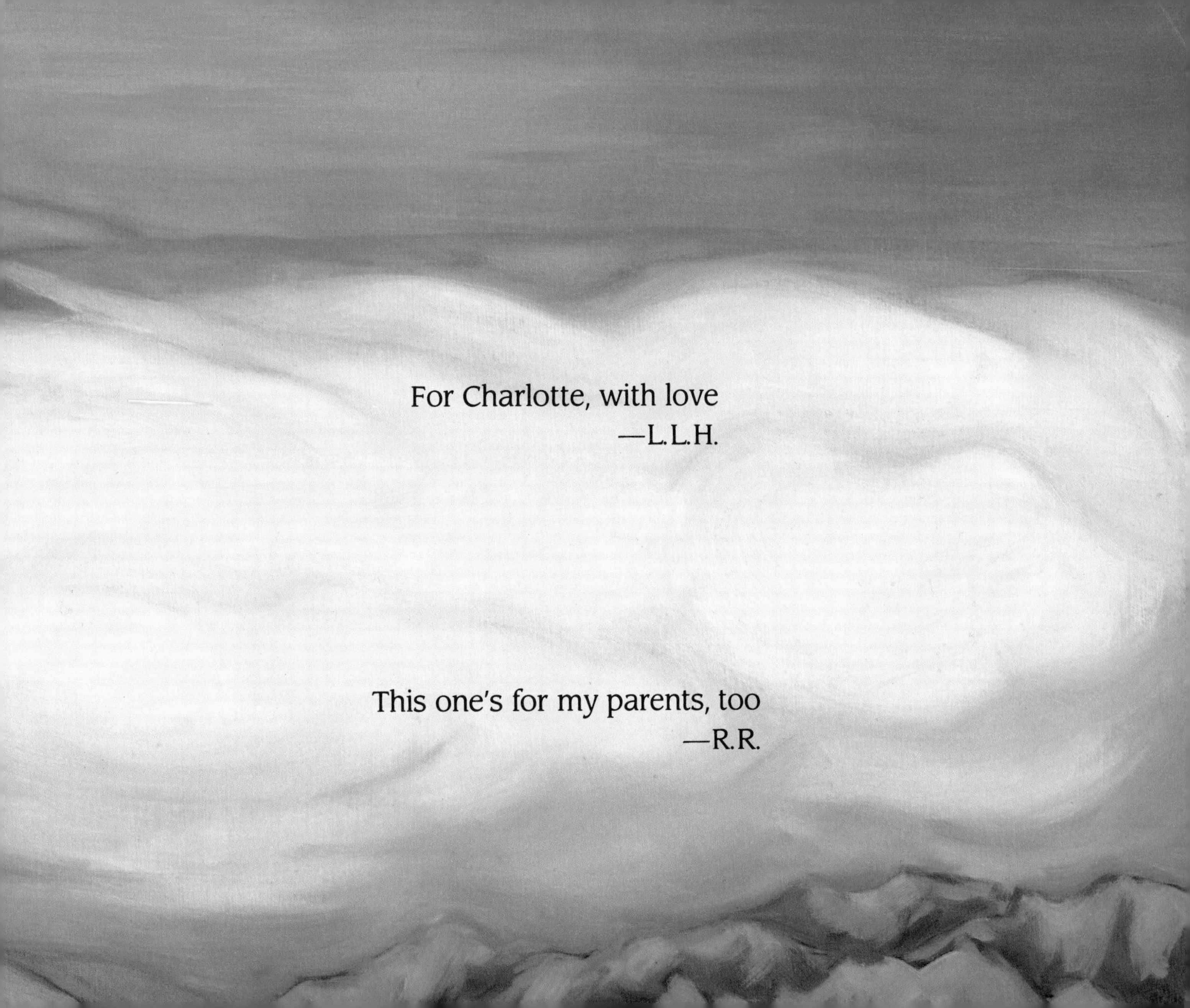

For Charlotte, with love

—L.L.H.

This one's for my parents, too

—R.R.

This little owl woke one foggy morning
and did not know where he was.
"Whoo–whoo, where am I?"

"H–o–m–e! H–o–m–e! H–o–m–e!"
hooted the foghorn out at sea.

But the little owl did not know
where he was in the tall grasses.

The chickadee sang, "Chick–a–dee,"
and the bobwhite called, "Bob–white, bob–white."

The bees buzzing quietly in the sea roses
buzzed, "Home, home, home,"
and the blossoms nodded, "Home,"

and the foghorn hooted,
"H–o–m–e! H–o–m–e!"

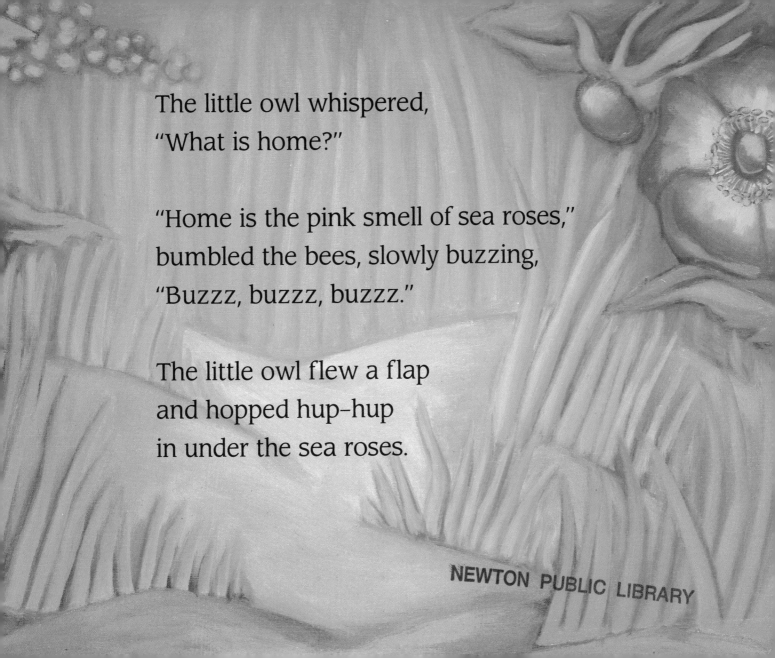

The little owl whispered,
"What is home?"

"Home is the pink smell of sea roses,"
bumbled the bees, slowly buzzing,
"Buzzz, buzzz, buzzz."

The little owl flew a flap
and hopped hup–hup
in under the sea roses.

A spider lay sleeping in the middle of her web,
and the little owl wondered aloud,
"What is home?"

"The center," whispered the spider, waking,
riding slowly on her silk.

"Buzzz, buzzz," buzzed the bees, "buzzz,"
and the blossoms nodded, "Home,"
and the foghorn hooted, "H–o–m–e!"
and the little owl did not know where he was.

He hopped hup–hup up onto the rocks.
Below he heard a mother seal playing
with her pups, humming quietly, "Home, home."
The little owl called out to the sea, "What is home?"

"Me and the sea," sang the mother seal.
"Sea rolling
    bell tolling
        flipper flapping
            waves lapping,"
barked the little seals.

"The center," whispered the spider.
"Buzzz, buzzz," buzzed the bees, "buzzz,"
and the blossoms nodded, "Home,"
and the foghorn hooted, "H–o–m–e!"
and the little owl did not know where he was.

He hopped hup-hup-hup
down into the sea grass.

A fiddler crab scuttled away.
A butterfly fluttered by.
Now a little breeze began to blow,
and the fog began to turn yellow.

The little owl saw
two brown snails
digging in the sand.
"What is home?" he asked.

"Our home is always with us,"
said the snails.

Overhead a loon laughed, "Loo–hoo–hoo–hoo–hoooo!"
"Home," called the little owl up to the sky.
"What is home?"

 "Loo–hoo–hoo!" laughed the loon.
"In my laugh I am home."
"In my flutter," said the butterfly.
"In my scuttle," said the fiddler crab.

"In my swoop," sang a swallow,
swooping and singing,
"swoop–low, swoop–low."

But the little owl did not know
how to flutter, or how to scuttle,
or how to laugh like the loon,

or swoop like the swallow.
He did not know where he was in the fog.

He hopped hup–hup out onto the wide sand.
A fish hawk hunting its breakfast
circled and cried, "I am home in my dive."

"In our quack–quack–quacking,"
quacked the eider ducks.
"In our lap–lapping," lapped the waves.

"In my fire," sang the sun,
rising higher and turning
the fog a bright, warm yellow.

The little owl hopped hup–hup
back into the tall grasses.
"I want my *own* home," he said.

Suddenly, then, the foghorn stopped hooting.
In the quiet the sun shone brightly,
and the little owl

saw his own mother beside him.

"Silly little owl," said his mother, "you *are* home."

He hopped hup–hup in under her open wing.

"In my flutter," whispered the butterfly.

"In my scuttle," said the fiddler crab.

"In my swoop," sang the swallow.

"In my hup–hup," sang the little owl,

and he hopped hup–hup–hup,

and he hooted,

"Whoo-whoo-whoo, I am home."